MR.MEN **LITTLE MISS**

MR. MEN and LITTLE MISS™ © THOIP (a Chorion Company)

www.mrmen.com

Mr. Men and Little Miss™ Text and illustrations
© 2010 THOIP (a Chorion company).
Printed and published under licence from
Price Stern Sloan, Inc., Los Angeles.

Original creation by Roger Hargreaves
Illustrated by Adam Hargreaves
First published in Great Britain 1998
This edition published in Great Britain in 2010 by Dean,
an imprint of Egmont UK Limited
239 Kensington High Street, London W8 6SA

Printed in Italy
ISBN 978 0 6035 6572 4

1 3 5 7 9 10 8 6 4 2

LITTLE MISS TROUBLE
MOVING HOUSE

Roger Hargreaves

DEAN

Little Miss Trouble lives in
Uptonogood Cottage surrounded by
fields and trees and more fields and
more trees, and even more fields.

Her nearest neighbours live miles and
miles away and there is a very good
reason for this.

That very good reason is Miss Trouble!

Nobody wants to live next door
to somebody who causes so
much trouble.

Somebody who telephoned Mr Lazy
at 5 o'clock every morning for a
whole week.

And somebody who told Mr Wrong that the best thing to use to polish his car was boot polish.

Now, because she lived all on her own, Miss Trouble found that she could not cause half as much trouble as she would like to.

What Little Miss Trouble longed for more than anything else was a neighbour.

One Monday when Little Miss Trouble was walking in the woods near her house she came upon a wishing well.

"Well, I never," she said, and then she had an idea. She threw a coin in the well.

"I wish I lived next door to ... somebody," she said out loud.

Later that day when she looked out of her window, she discovered that, as if by magic, which it was, her house was next door to Box Cottage, which is where Mr Chatterbox lives.

"Tee hee, now for some fun!" giggled Miss Trouble.

She crept down the lane, around the corner, up a telegraph pole and cut the telephone line!

Poor Mr Chatterbox.

No telephone.

No one to chat to.

But it was then that he looked out of the window and saw Miss Trouble's house.

Five minutes later there was a knock at Little Miss Trouble's door.

"Hello," said Mr Chatterbox. "Just thought I'd pop round for a quick chat. Funny thing, you know, my telephone's broken and ..."

And Mr Chatterbox talked and chatted and chatted and talked through the morning, all afternoon and late into the night.

The next day, Tuesday, a very tired Little Miss Trouble went back to the wishing well and threw in another coin. "I wish that I lived next door to someone else," she said.

And the very next morning Little Miss Trouble found herself living next door to Mr Bump.

She threw tiny stones at his window to wake him up. And smashed the window!

But Mr Bump has so many accidents that he did not notice one more broken window.

Little Miss Trouble went back to the wishing well.

On Wednesday Miss Trouble tried to play a trick on Little Miss Lucky. But she discovered that Miss Lucky is too lucky for any of Miss Trouble's tricks to work on her.

On Thursday there was nobody in at Little Miss Late's house.

She was late getting back from her holiday!

On Friday Little Miss Trouble told Mr Muddle that Mr Small had called him an egg-head.

But Mr Muddle got muddled up and instead of being angry with Mr Small he thanked him!

On Saturday Little Miss Trouble let the tyres down on Mr Forgetful's car.

But Mr Forgetful forgot he had a car and caught the bus.

On Sunday it was a very fed up Little Miss Trouble who returned to the wishing well to make a wish.

And then she had a thought.

A thought that went like this, "The trouble with neighbours," thought Little Miss Trouble, "is that they are too much trouble!"

And she went home and was very, very good and didn't make any trouble for anybody for ever and ever ...

... well, until Tuesday!